The Blessed
and The Damned

by

Sara Sheridan

Illustrated by Simon Manfield

First published in 2001 in Great Britain by
Barrington Stoke Ltd, Sandeman House, Trunk's Close,
55 High Street, Edinburgh EH1 1SR

Reprinted 2003, 2005

ISBN 1-842990-08-X

Printed in Great Britain by Bell & Bain Ltd

A Note from the Author

I never thought I'd end up writing, but it is the best job I've ever had and I'm planning to stick with it.

I got the idea for *The Blessed and The Damned* from my own background which is very diverse. My mother is Jewish and my father is Catholic. The whole family seems to have come from different parts of the world, but somehow we all met up. I liked the idea of writing a story about a gypsy girl who settles.

I love travelling. I live in Edinburgh with my daughter, Molly and we travel together whenever we can.

Look me up on http://www.sarasheridan.com

For Molly

20682

Contents

"After Dad's funeral ... I used to climb the hill..."

Chapter 1
Outsiders

It had been the worst year of my whole
life and now I'd lost everyone, everyone who
had ever made a difference. I wasn't open to
new ideas, that much was sure. I didn't
realise at first. I didn't notice the signs.

After Dad's funeral I lived on my own for
months. I used to climb the hill beside the
house and watch the MacBains with an old
pair of binoculars I found in the shed. I thought
I was doing it because I wanted to be reminded
that life could be normal.

I'd never had the kind of life that went on in the MacBain house. Their mother hadn't died when they were kids. They had proper mealtimes and set bedtimes. The three MacBain brothers stuck together no matter what.

But I discovered that this wasn't the real reason why I was watching their house. Though it turned out handy enough later to know exactly what they were up to at any hour of the day or night.

The real reason came to me one day as I lay in the bracken up on the hill. He was standing outside their house looking up at me and smiling, blond and hard-eyed. That was when I knew that everything that had happened to me was all *his* fault. Jason MacBain.

Jason had been in the same class as my brother Tom, and Tom would come home from school with these bruises on his arms where

2

Jason had pushed him up against one of the toilet doors and twisted the soft flesh hard.

"Get out, gypsy boy, you don't belong here," he'd sneer. Then he'd catch sight of me. "You too, Josie," he'd say.

Tom used to stand up to Jason. Once he even gave him a black eye. Tom was thirteen then and I was a year younger. The whole fighting thing didn't make any sense to me.

I was just a skinny, twelve-year-old girl and there wasn't anything I could really do to defend myself or him. I'd never fought anyone in my life. I was like a fisherman who couldn't swim – who knew he would drown if the boat sank. I knew if I had to fight I would lose anyway, so it was no good even thinking about it.

Up until then I was used to the fact that people picked on me. It seemed almost normal. Every day I used to walk across the playground and the group of girls who stood by the entrance would sneer at me.

"Dirty tinker," they would say loudly as I walked past.

After a while, when I didn't react, they got angry. They started to shout it louder every day until I could hear them from the other side of the playground. "Dirty tinker. Stinking gyppo."

And no-one did anything about it or tried to stop them.

The MacBains caused much more trouble for Tom than the girls ever did for me. Tom got wound up about it. One day, after school, as we were walking up to the bus stop Jason turned round and kicked Tom hard in the shins.

"What was that for?" Tom shouted.

Jason only smirked. "Motherless gyppo," he sneered. "Nobody cares about you."

I cared about him. I remember feeling really angry. I wanted to wait till the bus arrived and then push Jason MacBain in front of the huge, black wheels. I wanted the bus to roll over him slowly so his bones would crack one by one.

Jason strolled ahead and stood at the bus stop looking smug.

"Ignore him," I said to Tom, who had put his hand on my shoulder because he was limping.

It was difficult to ignore the MacBains though. The feud between them and us had been going on for years, since long before Mum died. I think it was going on before I was born. I'm not sure exactly how it started, but that doesn't really matter. What matters is that it went on and on. There seemed to be no stopping it.

Mr MacBain was a farmer and he had always wanted to buy our land to add to his own. But Dad would never sell it even though he didn't want to farm the place himself. Once my mother tried to work out some kind of agreement between them. Perhaps Mr MacBain could rent the land, or at least some part of it. I don't know. But it came to nothing and Mr MacBain left our house in a temper, his face as red as if he had been sitting out in the sun. "Lazy good-for-nothings," he had shouted, "living off the state!"

He was wrong about that. We weren't living off the state. Not that we let on about it to Mr MacBain. But we had our own money. Family money. Every week my father went into town and got some out from the bank. I had no idea where it came from and I didn't care much. I had more important things to worry about.

The July after Tom got so badly kicked at the bus stop, my father took me to judo classes. Tom wouldn't come. We stayed on the same traveller site for the whole of the summer that year, so that I could go every week. I developed into quite a little fighter. I hadn't realised how furious I was inside until I could finally do something about it and get my own back. Even the other tinker kids used to tease Tom and me whenever we stopped to park up at one of the Government Approved Gypsy Traveller Sites. My Dad was well known. And he wasn't liked in the gypsy community.

We were still on the site when one of the boys picked on me one day, after I'd had a few of those judo lessons. I floored him and then I kicked him in the stomach. Not hard, but hard enough. "That's a delayed reaction kick. It takes some time to work," I hissed, "but you should be dead in half an hour."

None of the others messed with me for the rest of the time we were there. When I got back to the farmhouse in October, the girls at school must have realised that there was something more confident about me. They didn't shout "gyppo" at me any more. They just ignored me.

Things were different for my brother, but then Tom was very different from me or anyone else.

For years before he killed himself we saw the signs of his craziness and we completely ignored them. Jason MacBain knew what was happening of course. He organised the daily bullying in the playground. Not so the teachers would notice. Just pushing and shoving, Tom's clothes ripped and his games kit missing. And the whispering behind his back.

My father didn't ask about the bruises on Tom's arms or why he walked with a limp from time to time. "That boy is talented, he has special gifts," he used to say over and over as if he were casting a spell that would save Tom from killing himself or seriously hurting someone else.

It really was a matter of which he would do first. Tom used to work out all kinds of insane ideas. He would shut himself away in one of the old outhouses at the back of the tatty, old farmhouse.

We lived in the farmhouse from October to April. We loved the wintertime – there was no central heating so we had open, peat fires. Around January the waterpipes used to freeze up. Then we'd have to walk down to the stream to collect ice so we could boil it to use for cooking. Or we would melt down the snow.

Things are different now – since my father died I have put in proper central heating. But in those days the pipes wouldn't thaw until March. Then at the end of the Easter term at the local school, my father would pack everything into the caravan and we'd take to the road. We never attended a summer term in our lives. The local council used to go mad – they didn't want that kind of thing going on in their area.

Once this really snotty guy from the Scottish Education Department came out to see Dad and talked about putting Tom and me into care. The whole works. Dad was really calm. He talked a lot about the Romany way of life and all that. He said that taking to the road was in our blood. The snotty guy looked doubtful. I mean, we were too pale-looking for the gypsy way of life. We didn't look right. But our people had always been Romanies. We were the real thing.

Anyway, Dad put on the full works about gypsy culture and tradition for the man from the Education Department. He settled him down in a chair with a mug of tea. Then he called me in and got me to recite poetry, great chunks of the stuff. I was thirteen I suppose. I loved T.S. Eliot and I could do most of *The Wasteland*. I've always had a really good memory.

After *The Wasteland* I did some Shakespeare – the bit where Ophelia gives up on Hamlet and the one from *Macbeth* where Lady Macbeth gives her husband hell and says that he isn't much of a man. There was a stunned silence when I'd finished. I was good at all that when I was a kid.

"Bring yer tea," Dad said then, breaking the silence. He took the snotty guy over the yard to the outhouse and showed him Tom's paintings.

They were beautiful, wild paintings of old stones up on the hill. I think only I could see that this is what they were. Tom just painted them as chunky blocks of colour in deep, dark oranges and vivid greens. Nightmare colours that used to wake him up screaming. Tom was a really great artist. I think he would have been recognised for that if he had lived.

"That boy is talented," my father murmured, sounding more sober than usual. "He has special gifts. You don't develop those gifts in houses or in schools. We're off travelling as soon as it's warm enough."

The snotty guy never came back.

"After that there was just the blackness ..."

Chapter 2
On The Road

When we were on the road everything was different. Because he couldn't bring all his painting gear with him, Tom took to science. He'd work out amazing experiments. One night we were camping on the West Coast and he climbed a cliff overlooking the ocean. I could make out the glow of his cigarette slowly mounting the hill above the campsite. It stood out in the deep, inky blackness. Tom was carrying something with him. I could tell

because if he had been walking empty-handed he would have moved with more speed and grace.

Tom's body had a natural rhythm to it which was attractive. Perhaps that was what got to Jason MacBain and made him so mad. All the girls in their class wanted to be around Tom.

Well, anyway, he didn't climb up the hill as he normally would – his movements were jerky. Then, when he got to the top, the cigarette went out and after that there was just the blackness. I sat up in my sleeping bag next to the window of the caravan and held my breath because I knew that he was

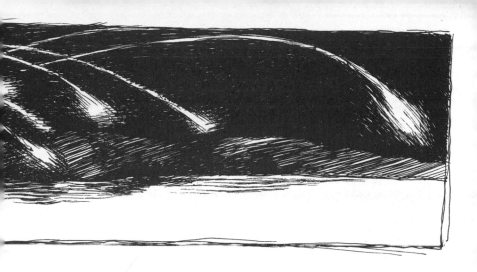

planning something. I pressed my nose up against the cold window then all at once there were sparks in the sky like a great waterfall flowing off the edge of the cliff and into the sea. It was beautiful. The sparks lit up the rockface behind which looked like a secret cave in the sudden burst of light. It was so unexpected that I cried out. Then I forced myself to be quiet and caught my breath.

Dad was already asleep. I could hear him snoring in the other room. He'd had half a bottle of whisky as usual and nothing would wake him now. Still I didn't want to make too much noise, just in case.

Tom's fantastic display went on for five minutes or so and then it suddenly stopped. Twenty minutes later he came back to the caravan. I was in the kitchen making hot chocolate on the old stove. I held a steaming mug out to him and he grabbed it from me.

"Josie," he said, his cheeks rosy and his eyes bright, "that was fantastic, babe," and he swung me round without spilling a drop from his mug.

"How did you do it?" I asked.

Tom slumped onto one of the flimsy kitchen chairs. "Fivepints," he said.

Fivepints was the dried milk we used instead of the real thing. It came in these plastic bottles and if you added water you got, well, five pints of milk.

"Burns really well. Sparks and everything," said Tom. "I only read the ingredients the other day and then I realised what I could do with it."

Tom's scientific experiments weren't always so beautiful to watch though. There was the day he tried to murder Jason MacBain's Dad, for example.

Now I can't really say I blame Tom for what he did. Jason had bullied him for a long time before he hit back and old man MacBain had hardly been a decent kind of neighbour. If Mr MacBain had only been polite to him I'm sure Tom never would have planted the bomb.

Tom was always a bit paranoid. More than a bit. He really thought people were out to get him. As a kid he used to check all the cupboards in his room before he would go to sleep. As he got older, after Mum died, the people he feared wore uniforms or dark suits – policemen, doctors, lawyers.

By his mid-teenage years, just before he died, he thought almost everyone was plotting against him – secret government agencies and big businessmen wanted to kill him. He was just mad. He stopped eating things that he didn't pick or grow himself. He said you never could be sure what was really in them.

That was how the problem started. It was the year after the Fivepints incident. The MacBains kept a few cows and Tom had gone off to ask Mr MacBain if he could buy some fresh milk – he wanted it untreated before any of his imaginary enemies could get their hands on it.

The old guy went ballistic and swore at him to get out. Blew him out of it. He took the big shotgun down from over the door and chased Tom back over to our side of the boundary line. He thought Tom was setting up a trap for him. It turned out selling untreated milk was illegal.

Tom was bitter and angry. We should have realised just how dangerous he was when he was in this state. I still can't believe he set up a bomb in the MacBain's cowshed. He somehow got hold of some potassium – it was no big deal – he probably nicked it from the school lab. And then he got hold of some acid, nitric acid or hydrochloric acid or something. Anyhow, he balanced the potassium above the door of the cowshed. When you opened the door the potassium fell into the bucket of acid and kaboom, there'd be a massive explosion.

Well, it should have gone kaboom. Poor Tom hadn't worked it out right. The potassium shot sideways and hit the floor instead of going into the bucket and Mr MacBain hit the roof and he chased Tom all over the place with three big dogs and a shotgun. There were bullet holes in the caravan windows where old man MacBain had fired at Tom and missed. It was months before Dad got round to having them fixed.

Tom wasn't sorry in the least. The next day he sat on the step in front of the outhouse and muttered to himself about how poisonous fumes under the guy's bed would have done the job much better. Perhaps permanganate, he mused. It was scary.

Looking back on it, he was really sick. He was wildy unstable. We should have sent him to Art School and he would have become famous. Or even to New York and he would have made a fortune. It's full of crazy people. But instead he stayed with us and got worse and worse.

At the end of that winter, I was sixteen and Tom was a year older. He spent days on end over in the outhouse painting. Those paintings were amazing. Like early cave paintings, you know. They had real soul in them.

Tom was working like a maniac. Every so often he'd come back to the house to eat, and he kept going on about the American artists and how the US Intelligence Service helped them to become famous. That part was true. I know because I read it somewhere. Tom must have seen it too and that made him even worse. He decided that while the US Intelligence supported young American artists, they wanted to destroy up-and-coming British talent like him. He set booby traps all over the farmhouse and around his studio. "Bastards won't get *me*," he muttered.

There came a time when Tom stopped cooking his food. It was pretty grim. He'd just take fruit and vegetables and milk over to the outhouse and eat them raw – potatoes, carrots, onions, anything else that was about. He didn't even eat bread. One time when I brought him out a cup of tea, he looked at me strangely and I saw him throw it out of the window as soon as he thought I'd gone.

A couple of weeks after that he killed himself. He set up the whole studio, hung each of his beautiful pictures carefully on the rough, stone walls, and then he carefully tidied everything up. He soaked his brushes and swept the floor. Once he had done all that he slit his wrists and bled to death right in the middle of it all.

Dad found him in the morning. He called to me and I ran over the yard in a pair of old pyjamas and nothing on my feet. I knew by the tone of Dad's voice that something awful had happened.

The low, morning light filled the old stone shed. Tom had taken out sections of the roof and had fitted glass panels, so that there would be enough light to paint by during the day. I just stood there looking round. His paintings were lit perfectly, I had never seen them look better. The colours glowed out.

It was then I realised, staring at the pale corpse of my brother in a pool of his own vermillion blood, that he had never used red in his paintings. Never.

And there was Tom, dead and white in the middle of the room, pale skin and a white T-shirt and a tatty, old pair of canvas trousers. Everything was soaked at the edges in his blood. My knees trembled and I fell to the floor. Dad stood in the doorway, his old, watery eyes looking even paler than usual. He didn't say a word.

That morning we dug a grave way up on the hillside behind the house and we buried Tom ourselves near the top of the slope which overlooks the MacBains' farm.

I knelt and wept on the cold mound of earth. I kept piling on more and patting it down. "You should have done something," I shouted at Dad.

Dad stayed silent. He didn't say anything at all. That had been the problem all along. He just stood there like some big, useless lummox and his blue eyes went on watering. He didn't have the guts to cry properly. I kicked him. I kicked him hard, right in his big, fat stomach.

"Why didn't you do anything?" I shouted.

Dad doubled up in pain, but he didn't even move to defend himself.

In the end he lumbered back slowly down the hill. I mumbled some kind of prayers which were running around my head. I spoke to Tom. "Why did you leave me?" I whispered, my hands caked with earth. "Come back." I was just a kid.

"At dawn I crept up on the hillside ... building a cairn ..."

Chapter 3
Covering Up

That night the house was silent and cold. Dad slept in his chair as usual, the empty bottle beside his empty hand. It had been that way since Mum died. I didn't sleep at all.

At dawn I crept up the hillside and I spent the whole morning building a cairn, just like the ones that Tom used to paint. I dragged big stones from all around and balanced them until the tower stood six feet high – taller than I was.

Then I crouched at the base of the stones and I cried and cried. Dad woke up after midday. I saw the lights turn on in the kitchen as he went through to make himself a cup of tea. Then the back door opened and he moved out shakily into the yard.

"Josie," he shouted.

I crouched silently up on the hill. Let the old man sweat, I said to myself as I huddled in to the stones. When it got dark I went down though. It was getting too cold.

"You know, they'll want to know what happened to him," I said to Dad. "We should tell someone. Get a death certificate or something."

This shocked Dad. I mean, I really think it hadn't occurred to him that he had to report Tom's death. We belonged to him, you see. Like dogs or cattle or anything else you might own. "We can say he went to London," he said. "We can say he ran away. They'll only make a fuss. They'll want to know what happened."

I knew what my Dad was really scared of. He was over six feet tall and he was broad. A big, strong man. But he was afraid of what he might have to *say*, of what people might *say* to him. I was too grief-stricken to care about that myself. But then I had only been ten when my mother died. I hadn't had to deal with the aunts and uncles who had all turned up for the funeral. I hadn't had to think of anything to say back when Mrs MacBain said it had probably been for the best. I hadn't even had to watch Mum's coffin disappear into the pit in the churchyard.

Maybe Dad just couldn't face all that again. I understand it better now. At the time I thought he was just a coward.

"You don't care," I screamed. "You don't care."

Dad's eyes narrowed. He was trying to show me that he did really care.

"There's nothing any of us can do now anyway," he said bitterly. "There's nothing to be done."

I burnt the outhouse to the ground. All of Tom's beautiful paintings. Every one.
Dad had to drive up the road and get the fire brigade, but by the time they got all the way to our place, everything Tom had cared about was burnt to the ground. The blaze didn't spread, although parts of the main house were smoke damaged. That was all. It was two in the morning by the time the fire engines left.

Dad was furious. He dragged me upstairs by my hair and he locked me into my room. At least Dad showed me some real feeling for once. I must have fallen asleep on the floor up there. He left me there for the whole of the next day. I thought about climbing out of the window, but I didn't get round to it. I just lay on the bed and thought about what had happened and about why it had happened.

I suppose that I partly blamed myself. You're not supposed to do that. But I did. I mean, Dad was useless and always had been. He didn't have a clue. But I should have tried to help Tom. It's not that we didn't talk or do things together. We spent our lives with each other. No, it was just that I should have listened to him more when he was going on about the US Intelligence Service and the food chain. I should have talked to him. I could have tried to calm him down. I could have kicked up a fuss at school and made them do something about Jason MacBain and his relentless bullying. I should have done something myself.

Dad wouldn't have done anything, of course. My father could talk about the Romany way of life and its culture. He could talk about freedom and the Scottish spirit.

29

But that was about all he could talk about. I was desperate for someone to talk to but there was just nobody there.

I stayed in my room all day. I stared out of the window for a couple of hours when it got dark. Up here it gets really dark – there aren't any streetlights of course. The night fell like a velvet blanket which muffled everything. Once or twice I saw the glimmer of some headlights a mile or so away, but mostly it was just blackness. The MacBain farm was hidden behind the hill and no-one else lived within eight miles of our place. I knew that no-one would ever know what happened to my brother.

"He drank more than ever ..."

Chapter 4
All Alone

That summer it was hot. It was the first time I could remember being at home when the sun shone all day. At first I thought that we would go off travelling like we always had. But by May the caravan was still parked in the courtyard in the blistering heat. Its dark windows were like blank, accusing eyes. We weren't going anywhere.

Dad pulled his tatty, old armchair out from the house onto the paving stones in the yard and he drank more than ever. The more he drank though, the more he sweated the alcohol out. His pale skin turned pink and his fat stomach glistened whenever I caught sight of it under his damp, blue shirt.

Instead of his weekly visits to town he started going every two weeks. He drew double the money out of the savings account and arrived home with two large boxes of tinned food, bags and bags of biscuits and fourteen bottles of Bell's whisky.

By June I hardly ever came back to the farmhouse. I camped out instead, sleeping under the stars on the other side of the woods. I used to check on the MacBains from time to time. I prowled round my territory like some kind of animal.

I watched Jason and his brothers checking the fields of flax and weeding out the barley. I watched Mrs MacBain up on a ladder making repairs to their roof. I saw Mr MacBain staring over at our land – which ran down to the sea in one direction and stretched out to the hilltop in the other. The boundary with his land ran down the side. Maybe he would have come over again to talk to Dad if things hadn't changed. Maybe.

When Dad died it seemed too peaceful. I came home one morning and there he was with his eyes closed, lying in his chair. He'd died the night before. Although he had sat there for the past week without saying a word and without moving, I knew right away, even from a distance, that something was wrong. He looked just too peaceful.

They sent an ambulance from town for the body and we buried him in the graveyard at the local church beside my mother.

It was only then I found out about Mr MacBain. As I turned away from Dad's flowerless grave, crying as quietly as I could, I read the name on one of the flowers laid out

on the new grave next door. Then I realised.
Strange that they had been such enemies in
life and yet so close in death. Jason's father
had a heart attack the day after Dad.
So there they were, buried side by side up at
the church. Strange really. I hadn't been
invited to the MacBain funeral. They didn't
come to Dad's. But I remember thinking that
at least that was the feud over and that was
something. Dead and buried.

"Our home ... had been bought by my great grandfather ..."

Chapter 5
Easy Target

Dad had made a will and since I was the
only one left everything was mine. The
house, the land and the bank account.
I checked through the deeds. I found out that
our home and its forty acres had been bought
a couple of generations ago by my
great-grandfather. He had made a fortune.
Travelled all his life. Had a way with horses
and made good bets. Years and years ago he
had bought the farm. He set up a high
interest account at the bank. There was
nearly seventy thousand pounds now. It had

passed from my great-grandfather to my grandfather, then to my father and now it was mine.

I held the savings book in my hands and sat in Dad's old chair beside the fire. I had had no idea. All that money. It seemed like a fairy tale – a fairy tale which had somehow gone wrong. Dad had died – but he had always been going to. You expect your Dad to die at some time.

But Tom was different. He was too young to die. If he had been alive we'd have shared the money together. I tried to think what he would have liked to do with it. Where we might have gone. What we'd have seen.

I wanted to do something special with the money. Everything up till then seemed so pointless – all that travelling in the summer and the long winter evenings at the farm. I wanted to do something I could be proud of. But I couldn't figure out what. Not all on my own. For weeks I kept the savings book in an empty Roses chocolates tin and I would go and check it three or four times a day, the pit of my stomach turning over as I read the bottom line. Seventy thousand pounds. It was a lot of money.

When autumn arrived I shut myself away in the house. I painted the rooms downstairs and had everything which had been falling apart since Mum died fixed. In the spring I looked over my land, trying to work out what the hell to do with it. There was Tom buried up on the hill. The rest of the fields were lying fallow, no crops, no animals, nothing.

People say the best land's in England but it was in Scotland that modern farming was really born. The land is great for it. The soil is rich and there's enough rain to make everything grow.

Dad had let the place go to wrack and ruin. You can't make a profit on forty acres.

It just isn't enough land. I didn't seem able to come up with any ideas. I watched the MacBain brothers working the soil on the other side of our boundary line. Their heart wasn't in it. If they went on like that they'd be broke.

A whole year passed and I was up on the hill staring at the MacBains place as usual when Jason came out of the house. There must have been something about him that day. He seemed different. And all of a sudden I knew that he stood for everything bad. All the crap things that had happened. Tom's death and Dad's too. And me being alone. The feud between our families. The misery of it all.

I began to shake and my heart was pounding. If Jason hadn't done what he did to Tom, I thought, there was just no way that I would be on my own. Jason MacBain had

pushed Tom right over the edge and turned him crazy. He'd started everything.
I remembered the day I'd imagined Jason being run over by the wheels of a bus. How good it would have felt to be planning my revenge.

Jason MacBain, and no-one else, was to blame.

My eyes narrowed in anger and then opened again in shock as Jason glanced behind him and then set off towards the hill. The track lead to only one place over that hill. To my house. We hadn't spoken in over a year. Something was going on.

I ran back towards my own front door out of his sight and reached it just as Jason was turning the corner of the yard. I glanced up with a shrug and shifted my weight from one foot to the other.

"Josie," he greeted me.

As I saw him close up I realised that he hadn't changed at all. His sandy hair was still cut really short. His hard eyes seemed to sneer as he spoke. He was too jolly by far – just the way he used to start with Tom. All friendly like this before he punched him hard.

"So sorry to hear about your troubles," Jason said. He smiled though his eyes were cold as he looked me up and down. "Well, you have grown up," he drawled.

"What do you want?" I asked, standing my ground, staring him right in the face.

Jason looked around just to make sure that no-one was close by. He used to do that behind the sheds at school right before he'd grab Tom by the arm and force him to the ground. I tensed up ready to fight if I had to, but Jason just leant towards me and whispered. "I want your land," he said. "I want to buy it."

"It's not for sale," I replied.

Jason waited for a second and nodded as if he had expected my answer. As if it was all part of his plan. "You're on your own, Josie. The nights are dark. There's no-one about if anything happens," he said.

But I wasn't going to let him scare me. I'd had enough of that.

"Oh, I've plenty of company," I said. "A really big dog and a shotgun."

And then I turned tail and strode into the house. I slammed the door behind me.

From the window upstairs I could see Jason MacBain making his way back over the hill.

I got the gun out of the attic. After Dad died I had been tempted to hand it in to the police. Now I was very glad that I hadn't. As darkness fell, I checked all the windows and

double-locked the door. Then I took the dog
to bed with me and I slept.

"The battle was on again ... I knew what Jason could do ..."

Chapter 6
No Surrender

The battle was on again. I knew that. Jason and his brothers were over at their place planning how to get me out.

It had to happen this way really. Their mother had gone to live with her sister and there were just the three of them. They'd had time to grieve for their father and take stock of their land. With my acres added to theirs they'd be able to earn enough money to make the farm pay. It was only logical. I was terrified. I knew what Jason could do. I'd seen what he did to Tom.

In the morning I walked up to the cairn where Tom was buried. That was the day before the Highland Fair. I knew the MacBains would all be going.

"Tom," I said, and my voice sounded strange because I didn't often go up there. Not to visit his grave. "Tom, that creep is back."

I sat down on the rough, damp ground and I stared down at the MacBain farm and I thought my brain was going to explode. I kept thinking about potassium and acid bombs and permanganate fumes under the bed. I thought about blowing up the flock of seagulls which came to rest on one of the fallow fields on the other side of their farmhouse. Just as a warning. If you feed seagulls aspirin, you know, they really will explode. They are like rabbits and horses, you see. They can't vomit.

One thing was for sure. I wasn't moving from the farm. I wasn't selling up. I was getting ready to fight.

I sat there for a while, thinking about the awful things I could do if I put my mind to it. Just at that moment Jason MacBain came out of the farmhouse. He kind of paused as he saw me way up on the hill.

Then to my horror, he started to move towards me. He walked with a slow and deliberate step. I thought of moving away but it would have been an act of surrender, an act of retreat. So I just sat there watching him. It was our land, I told myself, and he was trespassing as soon as he set foot on it. But he kept on coming. Right across the scrub at the bottom of the slope and upwards, without catching his breath. He was fit. He was dangerous.

"Morning, Josie," he said. "Nice view. Nice hill altogether this. I was thinking you know, there is this bad blood between us. From school days and everything. I was thinking, it's stupid. Completely stupid. Girl like you, on her own. You deserve better. Why don't you just sell up, Josie? It would work out well for both of us. You name your price."

Of course, he didn't know why the cairn of stones was there. He didn't know Tom was buried right beneath us. Tom would be turning in his grave at the very thought of Jason buying the farm.

"You could buy yourself a nice flat in Glasgow," he said. "It'd set you up."

"I don't like Glasgow," I said. "I like it here. I've lived here a long time and I won't be moving."

"Sure," said Jason. "Well, you might want to think about it, Josie. I don't want to scare you. But like I say, a girl on her own isn't safe. Certainly not if she's a gypsy." He strolled back down the hill again. I could see a threat in his every step.

I sat up by the cairn for a while. Jason got into his car and drove off towards town. I stared at the farmhouse and Jason's two brothers who were messing about down in the yard. I was biding my time.

Those MacBains stuck together. I leant up against the cairn and wondered what they had planned for me. It was just like being at school again, really, but this time I wasn't going to take it. The stakes were too high. If you give in from the beginning then you're lost. I knew that from experience. Tom's experience.

So I decided that there was nothing for it – I would have to take action at once.

"The bed lay unmade as he'd left it ..."

Chapter 7
Stalker

I walked back down to the house and, for
the first time since he died, I went into Tom's
bedroom. The room smelt musty. That was
to be expected though, because I'd never
aired it. The bed lay unmade as he'd left it,
only it was dusty and there was a pint glass
of dirty, grey water on the floor to one side.

I opened the window and I stripped off the
old bedclothes and laid them out for washing.
It was stupid, really, to have left it for so
long. Then I started to go through the

cupboards until I found what I was looking for. I had a plan.

I didn't kill them, if that is what you're thinking. I wouldn't have done that. I would have been bound to be caught besides. I could have killed them, though. That was really the point. It was like that kick with the delayed reaction that I gave the gypsy boy. It was a warning.

The genius lay in the threat of what *might* happen. It was the only advantage I had on my side. Along with the money in the bank and the fact that I'd watched them as long as I had. I'd seen the paint peeling from the window frames of the pretty, stone farmhouse, and I'd seen their old car slowly falling to pieces. I'd seen Jason's brothers half-heartedly baling up the hay, and taking their time over it. The MacBains needed money. That was my advantage over them. And I'd use it.

The next morning I climbed the hill again to look down on their land. It was a nice, little farm, really. They grew grain crops mostly – the government actually pays you for it. Oh, and flax. It was what had been keeping them going.

Anyhow, I watched for a little while because I wanted to check that they were all out at the Highland Fair. I checked out the scene carefully through my binoculars.

When I was satisfied that they'd all gone off I went over my plan one last time, patted Tom's cairn for luck, and then made my way down the hill to set things up. I was going to be ready for them when they came back.

I had never been in the house before, but I knew where I was going. Through the front door, up the stairs, checking each of the bedrooms and then hiding up in the attic. I would wait for them there.

I got up there around lunchtime even though the boys didn't get home until six o'clock. I had to be sure that I was stowed away well ahead of their return.

The MacBain brothers went to bed at ten. There had never been much movement around the house at night, no lights going on and off, no-one coming back late.

They went to bed early and slept soundly. I waited until eleven just to be sure. I listened carefully until all the movement had stopped and the breathing from each of the bedrooms was steady. Then I climbed carefully down the attic stairs and slipped into Jason's room at the end of the corridor.

I pulled some electrical tape out of the bag I had over my shoulder and I covered his mouth, so he couldn't make any noise. He woke up at once, of course, in a panic. I was sitting on the edge of his bed and he began to flay his arms around, but fresh from sleep it was an easy job to tie him down.

I had chosen Jason's room not only because he was the worst bully of them all, but also because he slept the furthest away from the others. His muffled shouts wouldn't reach down to the other end of the corridor. Anyhow, he stopped as soon as I showed him the knife.

"Right," I whispered. "This should be easy for you, Jason. All you have to do is listen.

"I just want you to know, you bastard, that my farm is my home. My family has lived there for a long time. We might have travelled, we might have gone away a lot. But it's our home. And I'm not a kid any more and I'm not crazy like my brother was. So if you try to frighten me, I'll frighten you right back. I'll destroy you and your brothers, make no mistake about that. It's a long way from anywhere here. Three nice guys like you. It's just too easy."

Jason's eyes looked frantic. I had the hunting knife which Tom had used for skinning rabbits when we were younger. It was sharp. I took a deep breath and smiled before I continued.

"Now I can do to your brothers what I'm doing to you any time I like. I have the guts to do it, make no mistake. We should never have been neighbours, Jason. And now I want to put that right. I'm going to turn the tables on you. I'm going to buy your farm. I'm going to make you a good offer. Either that or I shall make your life hell. Girl on her own like me. I don't have anything to lose, and you do.

"When you get up tomorrow morning and you think this is a dream, there's going to be an envelope with a letter in it on the kitchen table and you're going to take that envelope to your lawyer and tell him that you're selling this farm to me. And then you'll have six weeks to move out.

"You won't see me. I won't be at home. But I'll be somewhere that I can see you. You try to mess with me in any way, and any time of the day or night I'll be back and you'll regret it. When you move out you get a nice lump sum to split between the three of you. You understand?"

Jason nodded slowly.

"I'm a gypsy, remember?" I leant in close to his ear and whispered. "Well, you know what they say about us gypsies? You can consider yourself cursed if you do anything other than what you just agreed to."

Then I got a bottle of chloroform out of the bag, poured a little onto a handkerchief and held it over his mouth until he passed out.

"It was a good offer that I made them ..."

Chapter 8
Game Over

I didn't leave any evidence in his bedroom. It was tempting enough to cut him with the knife. Just one little nick on his arm or leg, to remind him that I meant what I had said. But it wasn't worth it. I couldn't leave any evidence or he could go to the police.

That midnight I burnt everything I had used that day in a rubbish bin in the yard. Then I went and slept in the woods. I took the binoculars with me. In the morning, from my hiding place, I watched them as they sat around the kitchen table. I saw them talking for ages, and then Jason got on the phone.

It was a good offer that I'd made them – all of grandpa's money and a bit more too. I'd raised a loan at the bank. With a hundred and forty acres I'd have enough land to be in profit. And they needed the money.

The MacBain boys moved out over the summer. They didn't stay around long. Someone told me that they split the money between them and moved to the East Coast. I got to harvest their crops as part of the deal, but do you know, I didn't enjoy it at all. I mean all of those government forms and you get more money not to grow things in the end than to grow them.

As winter drew on I patched up their old farmhouse. I rented it out as a holiday home. This year I've made a few more decisions and I'm switching crops. Flowers and herbs.

In memoriam, really. White heather for luck and rosemary for remembrance.

Which only goes to show you that I really am a gypsy at heart.

"With a hundred and forty acres I'd have
enough land..."

Barrington Stoke would like to thank all its readers for commenting on the manuscript before publication and in particular:

Sarah Blackie
Rachel Clifford
James Conquer
Lizzie Dixon
Lizzie Foote
Laura Harvey
James Hooper
Michael Huntly
Makayla Iveson
Sean Kilvin
Sam Lewis

Kenneth McCallum
Marion McKinnon
John Morris
Alexandra Patsalides
Leigh Ritchie
Natalie Sexton
David Taggart
Katie Taggart
Jack Vine

Become a Consultant!

Would you like to give us feedback on our titles before they are published? Contact us at the email address or website below – we'd love to hear from you!

Email: info@barringtonstoke.co.uk
Website: www.barringtonstoke.co.uk

More Teen Titles!